ABOUT THIS BOOK

The illustrations for this book were created digitally with handmade watercolor textures. This book was edited by Farrin Jacobs and art directed by David Caplan. The production was supervised by Kimberly Stella, and the production editor was Jen Graham. The text was set in Granjon LT Std, and the display type is Sofa Sans.

Remember to Dream, Ebere

by Cynthia Erivo

illustrated by Charnelle Pinkney Barlow

L B

Little, Brown and Company
New York   Boston

When it was time to go to sleep,
Ebere's mother always kissed
her on the cheek and said,
"Remember to dream, my love."

And when it was
time to go to sleep…

...Ebere usually had a
hard time staying asleep.

She often crept out of bed and
went looking for her mother.

"Mommy," she said one night,
"I had the most amazing dream.
I dreamed of a rocket ship!"

"Oh my. How big was this rocket ship?"

"I don't know," said Ebere.

"You'd better go back and dream some more."

And she did.

"Mommy, the rocket ship is as big as two houses!" Ebere exclaimed.

"That's wonderful. And what color is the rocket ship?"

"I don't know," said Ebere.

"Go back and dream, my love."

And she did.

"Mommy, the rocket ship!
It's as big as two houses—
and as red as a fire engine."

"That sounds wonderful. Does
the rocket ship have a name?"

"I don't know," said Ebere.

"Go back and dream some more, my love…

"…and dream it
in the biggest
letters ever."

And she did.

"The rocket ship
is as big as two houses
and as red as a fire engine—
and it's called *The Light Chaser*."

"That is a beautiful name, my love. It would be a shame for such a beautifully named rocket ship to have no captain. Who is the captain of the ship?"

"I don't know, Mommy.
I'd better go dream some more."

"Great idea."

"Mommy, I dreamed again, and guess what? *I* am the captain of the ship! I can go anywhere in the universe."

"My love, you are the
captain of all your dreams.
And I want you to have as
many dreams as you can—

"Just remember to always dream them as big as two houses, as bright as fire-engine red, and as bold as the name *The Light Chaser*."

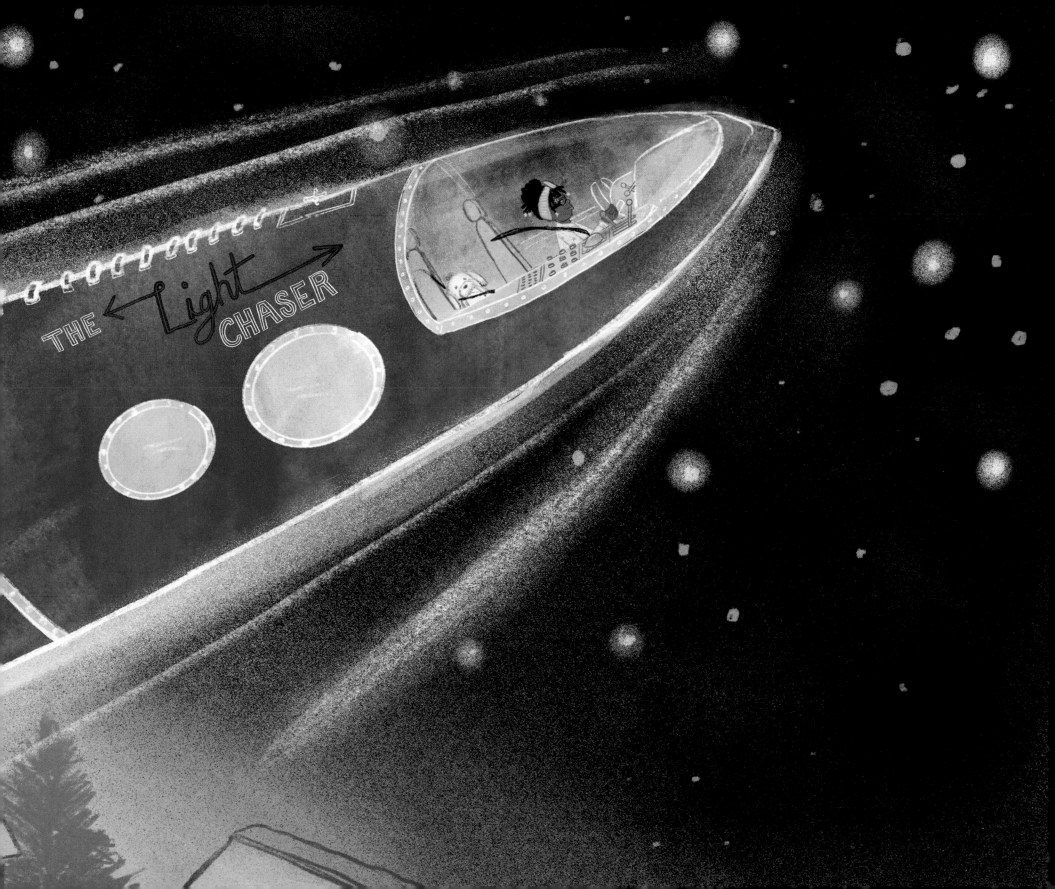